Sucked through a worm-hole . . .

to a strange, new place,

lost in a galaxy called Fairy Tale Space.

The SuperStar needs to refuel.

"This looks like a good place," says Ace.

Scout and Ace get in their space buggy.

A wombat comes racing by.
"What's the hurry?' shouts Scout.
"Is it a race?" says Ace.

Sorry, in a hurry.

But the wombat can't stop.
He races on.

A space-monster comes racing
after him.

It opens its mouth and swallows
the wombat. Just like that.

Scout and Ace race off.
But the monster races after them.

They race past a cat fast asleep on a mat.

But the cat doesn't scat.

So the monster opens its mouth
and swallows the cat. And the mat.

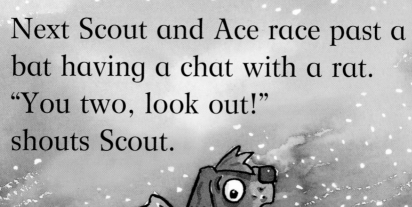

Next Scout and Ace race past a
bat having a chat with a rat.
"You two, look out!"
shouts Scout.

Too late. The monster opens its mouth wide . . .

. . . and swallows the bat inside. And the rat.

Finally, the space-monster catches up with Scout and Ace.

It opens its mouth very wide

and swallows them both inside.
And the space buggy.

Inside the monster's belly,
all the animals are still alive.

Scout can't see how to get them out.

But Ace has an idea . . .

He tells the animals to tickle
the monster's belly, which
makes the monster giggle

. . . and jiggle

. . . and wiggle

. . . and wriggle.

The monster starts to cough . . .

and wheeze and sneeze . . .

Until the wombat and the cat
and the mat

and the rat and the bat
and Ace and Scout all fly out.

And the space-monster flies
into space. Getting smaller . . .

and smaller . . .

and smaller.

Until it's just a spot . . .

then a dot . . .

. . . and then it's not.

The animals thank Scout and
Ace for getting them out.

They help them to find some fuel.

Then Scout and Ace head back to the SuperStar.

Ace says, "That space-monster's eyes were bigger than his belly. He should have stuck to jelly. Boom! Boom!"

Scout groans. Ace's jokes
are bad, but his verse is worse.
"Time to get out of here," he
says.

Fire the engines...

and lower the dome.

Once more our heroes...

are heading for home.

Enjoy all these stories about

SCOUT and ACE

and their adventures in Space.

Scout and Ace: Kippers for Supper
1 84362 172 X

Scout and Ace: Flying in a Frying Pan
1 84362 171 1

Scout and Ace: Stuck on Planet Gloo
1 84362 173 8

Scout and Ace: Kissing Frogs
1 84362 176 2

Scout and Ace: Talking Tables
1 84362 174 6

Scout and Ace: A Cat, a Rat and a Bat
1 84362 175 4

Scout and Ace: Three Heads to Feed
1 84362 177 0

Scout and Ace: The Scary Bear
1 84362 178 9

All priced at £4.99 each.

Colour Crunchies are available from all good bookshops, or can be ordered direct from the publisher:
Orchard Books, PO BOX 29, Douglas MM99 1BQ.
Credit card orders please telephone 01624 836000 or fax 01624 837033
or email: bookshop@enterprise.net for details.

To order please quote title, author and ISBN and your full name and address. Cheques and postal orders should be made payable to 'Bookpost plc'. Postage and packing is FREE within the UK – overseas customers should add £1.00 per book. Prices and availability are subject to change.

ORCHARD BOOKS, 96 Leonard Street, London EC2A 4XD.
Hachette Children's Books, Level 17/207 Kent Street, Sydney, NSW 2000.
This edition first published in Great Britain in hardback in 2005. First paperback publication 2006.
Text © Rose Impey 2005. Illustrations © Ant Parker 2005. The rights of Rose Impey to be identified as the author and Ant Parker to be identified as the illustrator have been asserted by them in accordance with the Copyright, Designs and Patents Act, 1988. A CIP catalogue record for this book is available from the British Library.
ISBN 1 84362 175 4   10 9 8 7 6 5 4 3 2 1
Printed in China